Dear parents, caregivers, and educators:

If you want to get your child excited about reading, you've come to the right place! Ready-to-Read *GRAPHICS* is the perfect launchpad for emerging graphic novel readers.

All Ready-to-Read *GRAPHICS* books include the following:

- ★ **A how-to guide to reading graphic novels for first-time readers**

- ★ **Easy-to-follow panels to support reading comprehension**

- ★ **Accessible vocabulary to build your child's reading confidence**

- ★ **Compelling stories that star your child's favorite characters**

- ★ **Fresh, engaging illustrations that provide context and promote visual literacy**

Wherever your child may be on their reading journey, Ready-to-Read *GRAPHICS* will make them giggle, gasp, and want to keep reading more.

Blast off on this starry adventure . . . a universe of graphic novel reading awaits!

Geraldine Pu

and Her Lunch Box, Too!

Written and illustrated by Maggie P. Chang

Ready-to-Read *GRAPHICS*

Simon Spotlight

New York   London   Toronto   Sydney   New Delhi

For my Amah

SIMON SPOTLIGHT
An imprint of Simon & Schuster Children's Publishing Division
1230 Avenue of the Americas, New York, New York 10020
This Simon Spotlight edition June 2021
Copyright © 2021 by Margaret Chang
All rights reserved, including the right of reproduction
in whole or in part in any form.
SIMON SPOTLIGHT, READY-TO-READ, and colophon are registered
trademarks of Simon & Schuster, Inc.
For information about special discounts for bulk purchases, please contact
Simon & Schuster Special Sales at 1-866-506-1949 or business@simonandschuster.com.
Manufactured in the United States of America 0521 LAK
2 4 6 8 10 9 7 5 3 1
Library of Congress Cataloging-in-Publication Data
Names: Chang, Maggie P., author, illustrator. Title: Geraldine Pu and her lunch box, too! /
written and illustrated by Maggie P. Chang. Description: Simon Spotlight edition. |
New York : Simon Spotlight, 2021. | Series: Ready-to-read. Level 3 | With encouragement
from her supportive lunch box, a young girl ignores a classmate's teasing and heartily
enjoys yellow chicken curry, stinky tofu, and other tasty lunches prepared by her Taiwanese
grandmother. Identifiers: LCCN 2020038696 (print) | LCCN 2020038697 (ebook) |
ISBN 9781534484689 (paperback) | ISBN 9781534484696 (hardcover) |
ISBN 9781534484702 (ebook) Subjects: LCSH: Graphic novels. | CYAC: Graphic novels. |
Ethnic food—Fiction. | Food—Fiction. | Lunches—Fiction. | Lunch boxes—Fiction. | Taiwanese
Americans—Fiction. Classification: LCC PZ7.7.C419 Ge 2021 (print) | LCC PZ7.7.C419 (ebook)
| DDC 741.5/973—dc23 LC record available at https://lccn.loc.gov/2020038696 LC ebook
record available at https://lccn.loc.gov/2020038697

Contents

How to Read This Book

This is Geraldine. She's here to give you some tips on reading this book.

It's me, Geraldine! The pointy end of this speech bubble shows that I'm speaking.

When someone is thinking, you'll see a bubbly cloud with little circles pointing to them.

This box I'm inside is called a panel. On each page, read the panels from left to right...

...and top to bottom.

Ta-da! Now you're READY TO READ this book!

GURGLE GURGLE

Oops, those gurgles were the sound of my tummy grumbling. It's time to eat!

Hee-hee

Words from Geraldine's World

Geraldine and her family speak English, Mandarin Chinese, and Taiwanese. Mandarin Chinese and Taiwanese are both languages spoken in Taiwan. Some of Geraldine's family members used to live there!

 Amah (said like this: ah-MAH): the word for "Grandma" in Taiwanese.

Biandang (said like this: BEE-en-DONG): Geraldine's nickname for her lunch box. This is the Mandarin Chinese word for "Taiwanese lunch box," which is usually a yummy meal of rice, meat, veggies, and an egg all in one box.

 curry: the yellow curry in this story is a common and comforting dish that many Taiwanese people make.

bao: a bun that's white, soft, and filled with meat or vegetables or both. "Bao" sounds like "wow," and that is often what people say when they eat one!

 tofu: a food made of soybeans that can taste sweet, salty, spicy, or even stinky.

A note on the spellings in this book:
There are different ways to write Mandarin Chinese and Taiwanese words in the English alphabet, but our book spells them the way Geraldine likes to spell them.

Chapter One

Meet Geraldine Pu. Her last name rhymes with "blue" and "chew."

Geraldine loves her family,

her favorite things,

hair clip

pencil case

lunch box

and going to school.

The best part of school for Geraldine is...

...LUNCH!

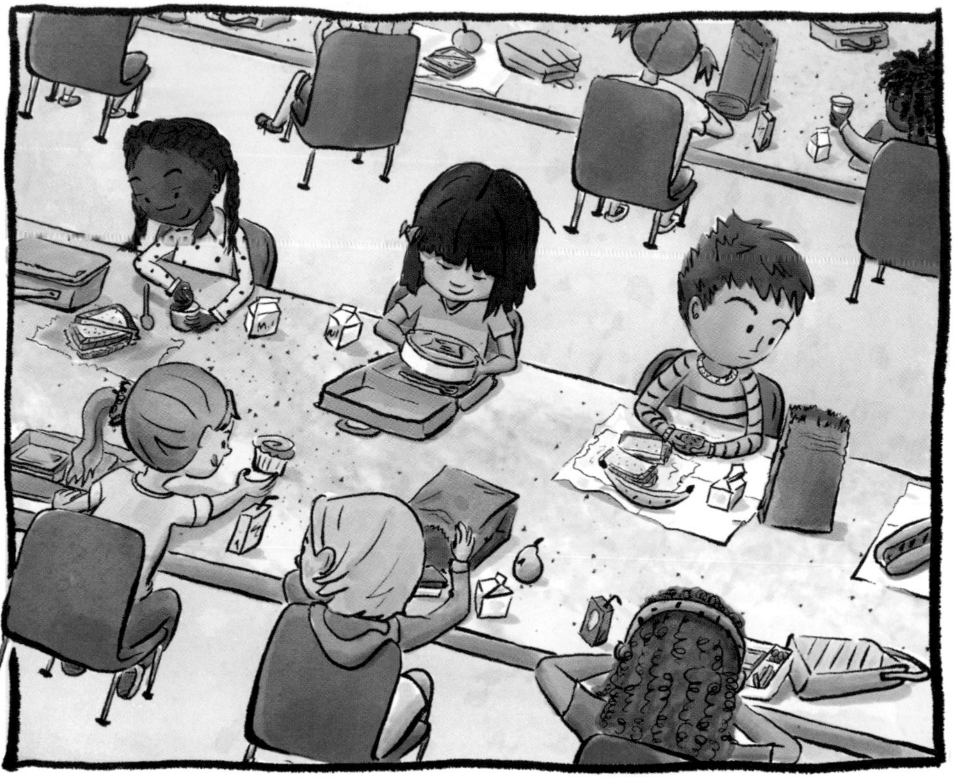

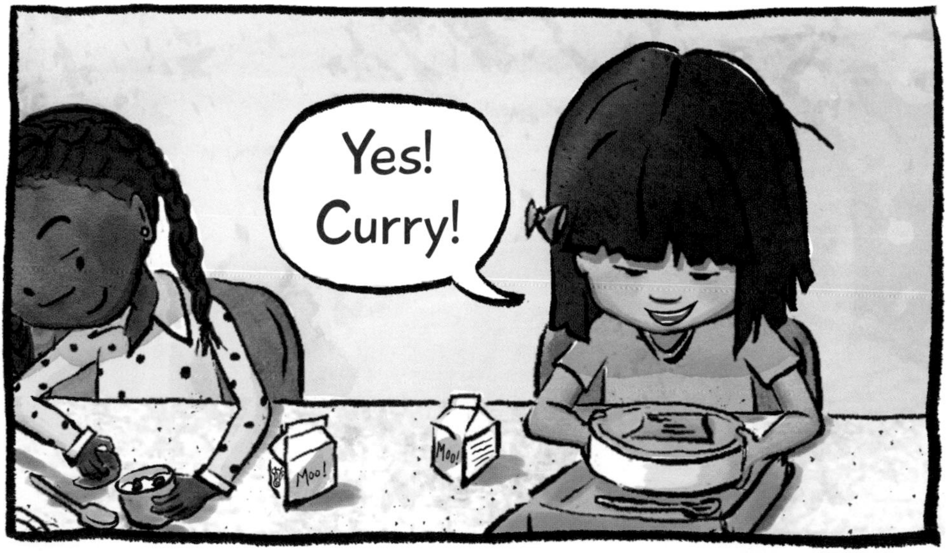
Yes!
Curry!
Moo!
Moo!

She LOVES the lunches Amah makes.
Amah even includes notes:

Do you know what else Geraldine loves?

ME!

Her lunch box.
She calls him Biandang
(said like this:
BEE-en-DONG).

She's decorated him
with stickers.

There's even one that reads:

That's right, and I have an important job to do!

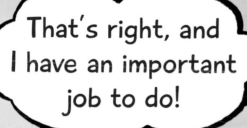

Biandang's job:

☑ Carry lunch

☑ Protect lunch

☑ Keep lunch from spilling everywhere

Every day Geraldine and Biandang take good care of each other.

Everything is great until...

...Nico arrives.

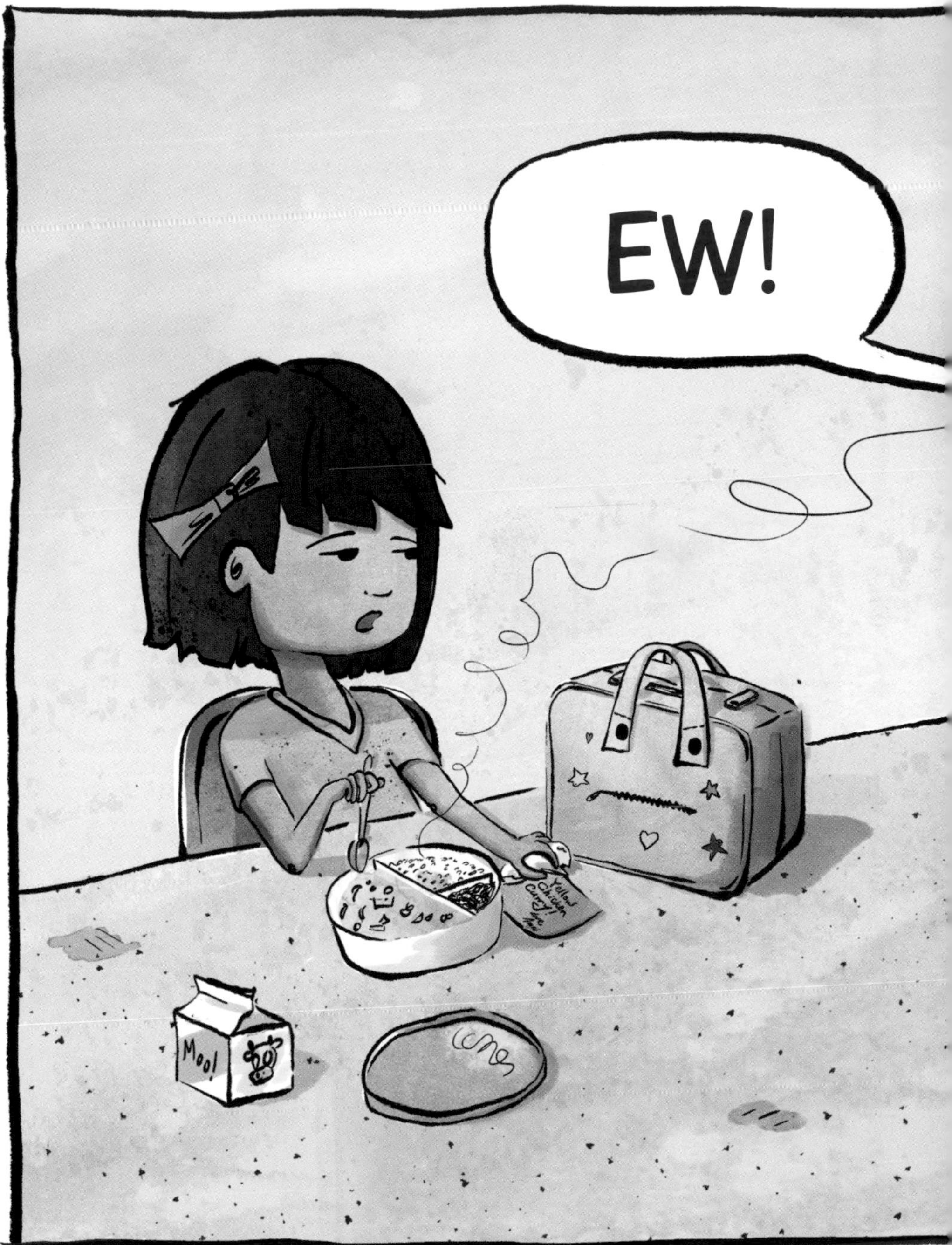

EW!
Yellow Chicken Curry!
Moo!

Nico is afraid of anything new.
Even curry.

He says things like:

Your lunch is GROSS!

Nico is new to Geraldine's lunch table.
Now his new ideas are catching on.

Ew, gross!

Ohh, yuck!

Yeah, so, SO weird!

Geraldine growls,

It's not THAT weird.
It's...delicious.

But that night she clutches Biandang tight as she asks Amah,

Can you pack me a sandwich for lunch tomorrow?

Hmm, we're out of bread... but I'll try.

Chapter Two

The next day at lunch Geraldine opens Biandang and finds...

...something that does NOT look like a sandwich!

Amah's note explains.

Nico sees the bao and asks,

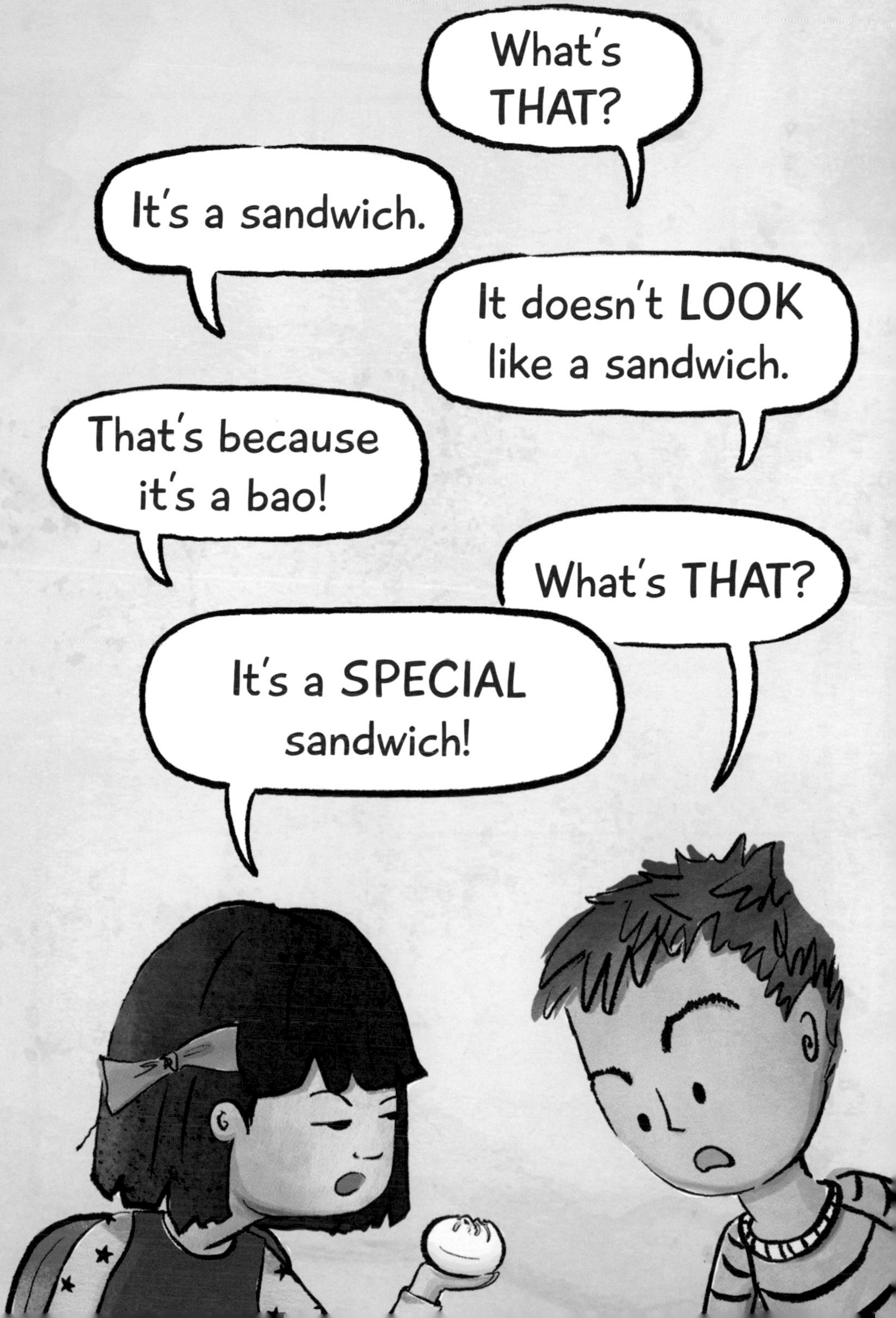
What's THAT?
It's a sandwich.
It doesn't LOOK like a sandwich.
That's because it's a bao!
What's THAT?
It's a SPECIAL sandwich!

Geraldine decides to pack Biandang back up.

She doesn't even take a bite of the bao.

By late afternoon Geraldine's tummy begins
to grumble.

This distracts her so much, she leaves
Biandang on the bus by mistake.

Luckily, Deven notices.

He hollers,

But others notice too, like Nico.

Even if they don't mean for Geraldine to hear, she hears.

So when she gets home,

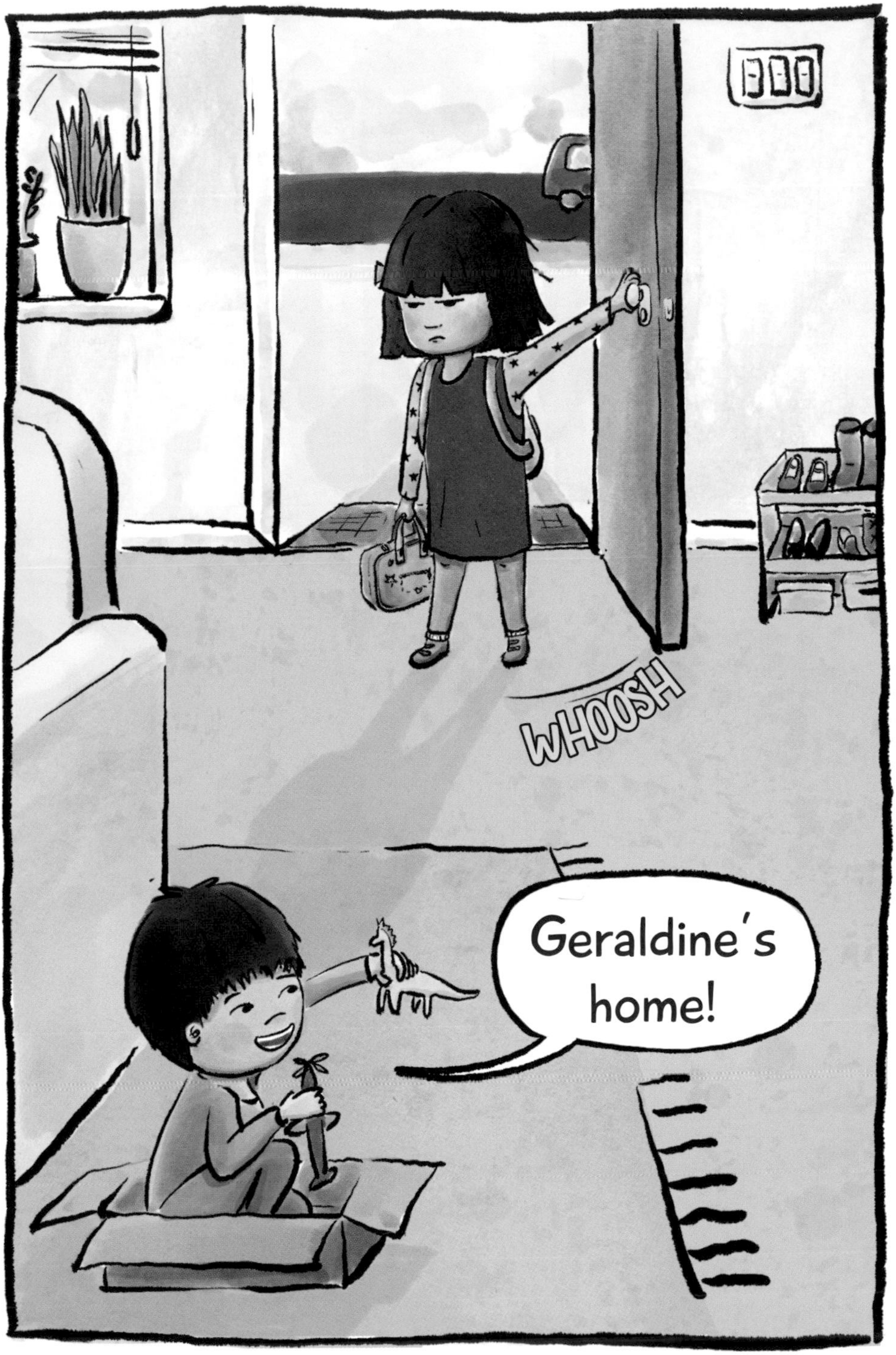
WHOOSH
Geraldine's home!

she takes off her shoes,

stomps up the stairs,

slams her bedroom door,

and then...

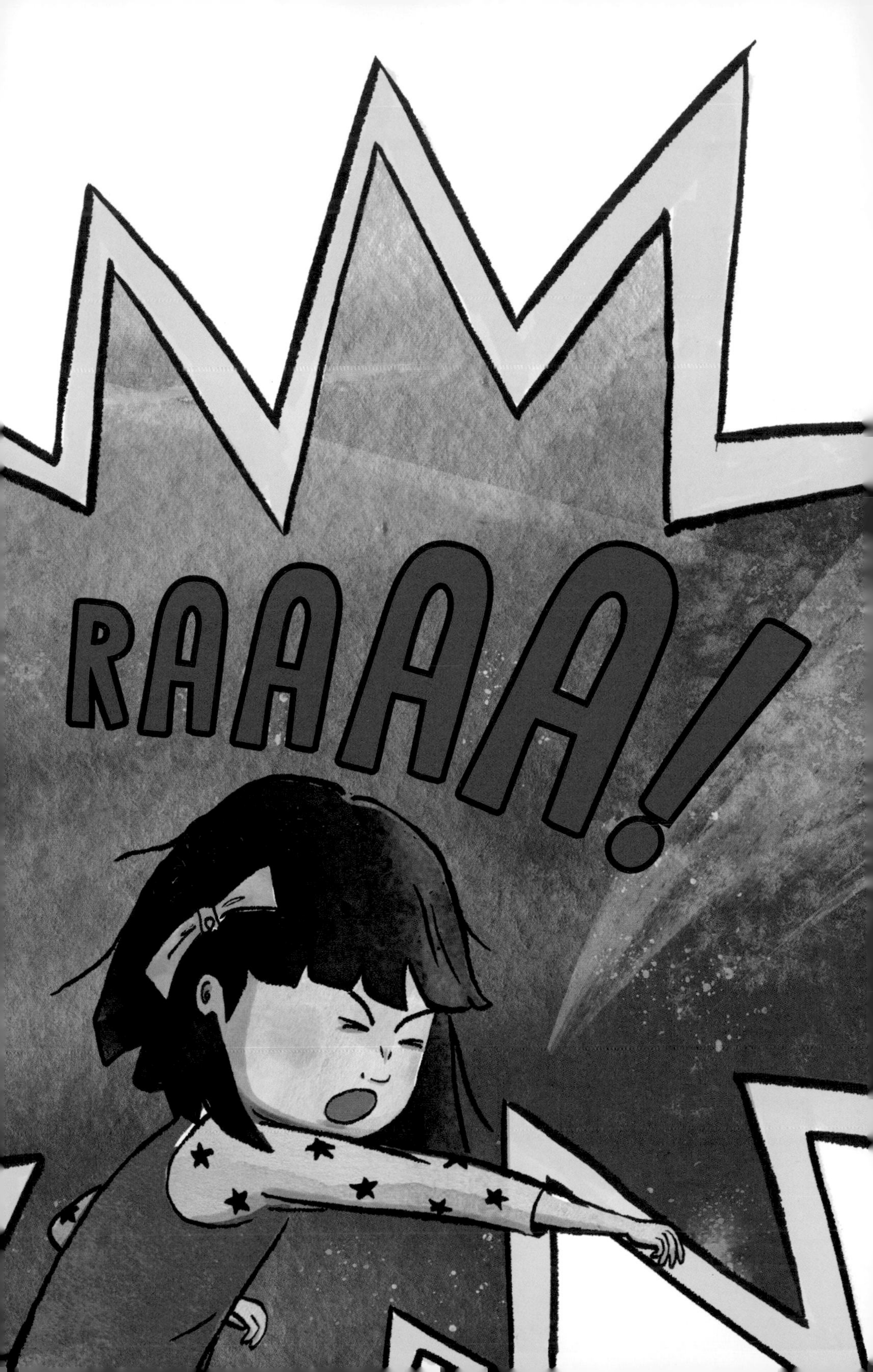
RAAAAA!

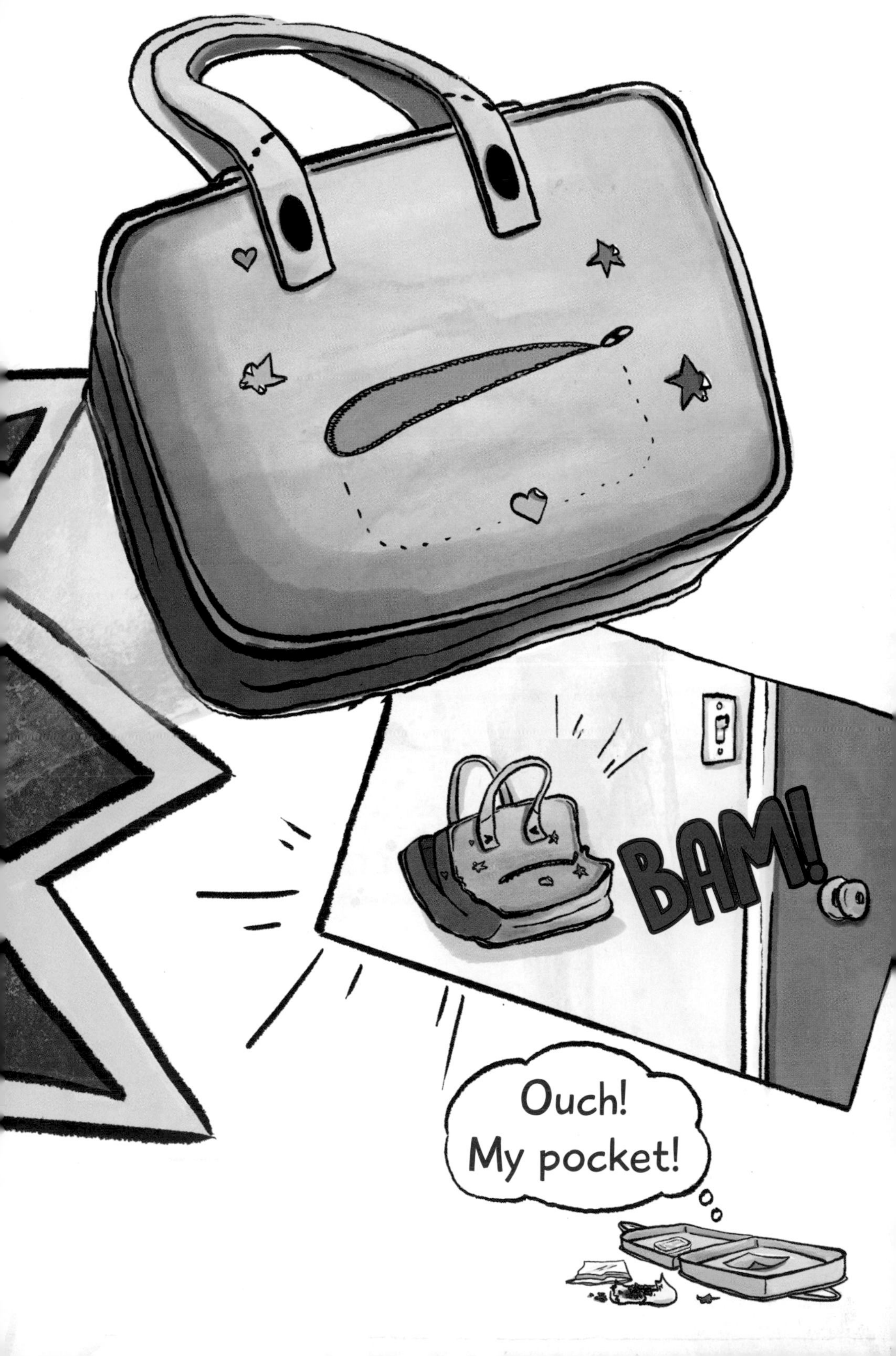
BAM!
Ouch!
My pocket!

Geraldine gasps and rushes to
Biandang's side.

She fixes his stickers and glues his pocket.

This makes her feel better.

33

But Geraldine hates that
she wasted her bao.
Even with lint, it looks so
yummy to her.

I should have
just eaten it.

Just then Amah calls from downstairs,

Geraldine, where's your Biandang?

Geraldine doesn't want
Amah to know she
didn't eat her lunch!

She tosses the bao into the
garbage and sighs.

Chapter Three

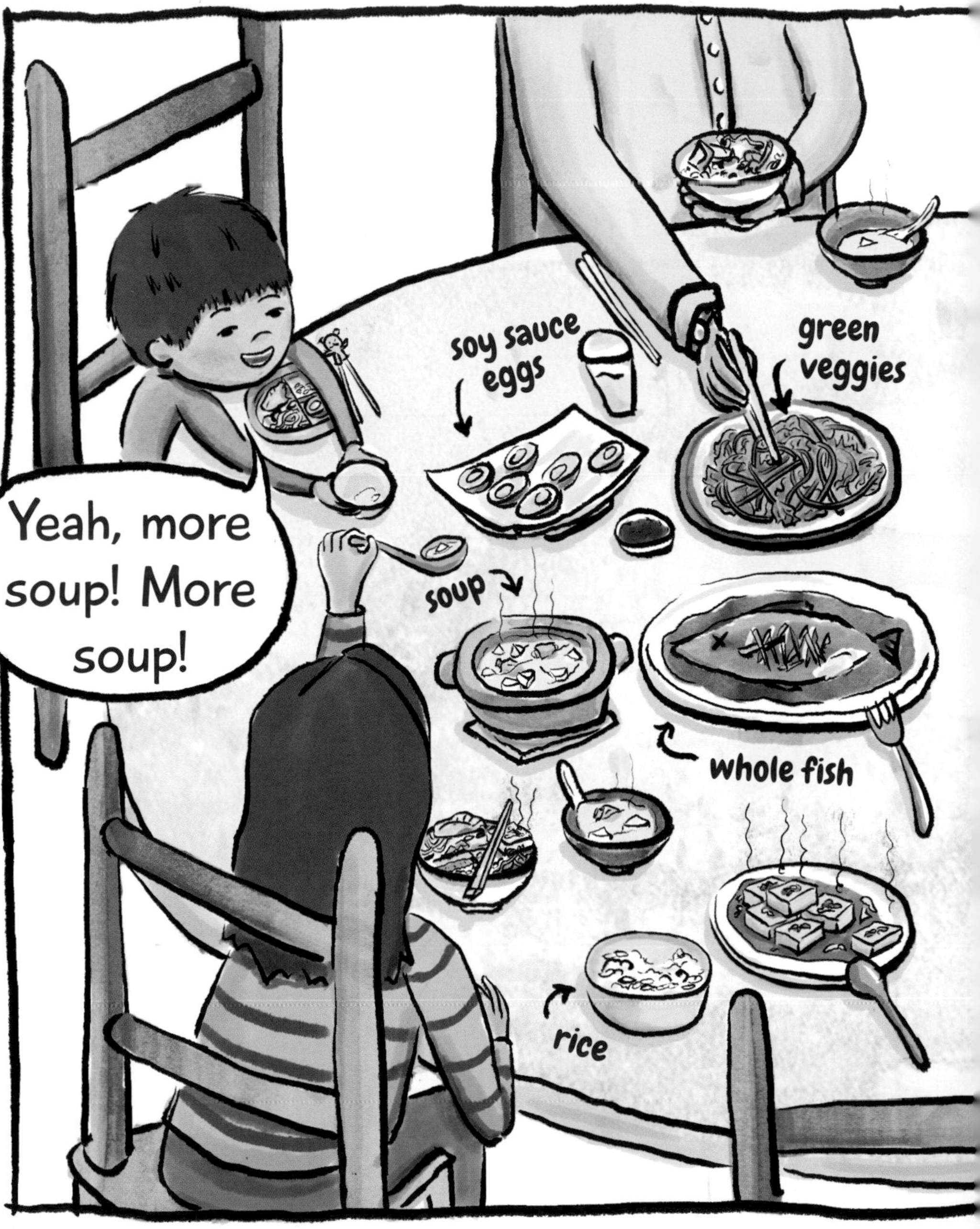

soy sauce eggs
green veggies
Yeah, more soup! More soup!
soup
whole fish
rice

That night with her family, Geraldine eats from every dish at dinner.

So juicy, Amah!

dumplings

noodles

cucumber salad

pork chop

There's even a super smelly dish with a super silly name: **stinky tofu**.

Afterward Amah asks,

Geraldine, do you want leftovers for lunch tomorrow?

Stinky tofu—maybe it is not as good as today's bao, but it is too good to waste!

Um...uh...ok.

Geraldine finally replies.

But later she begins to worry about lunch.

She thinks about it for a long time.

The next morning...

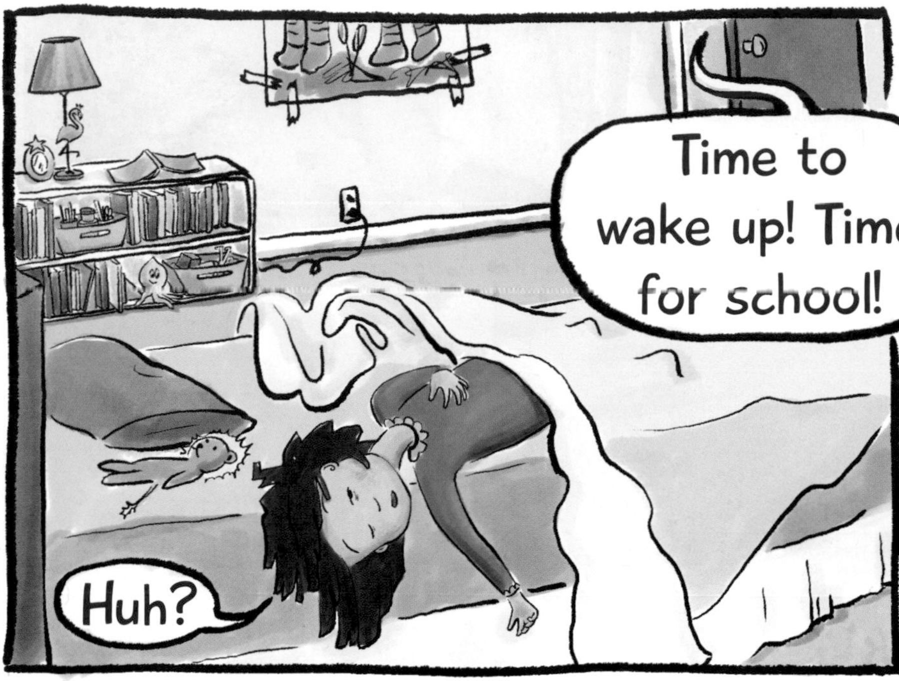
Time to wake up! Time for school!
Huh?

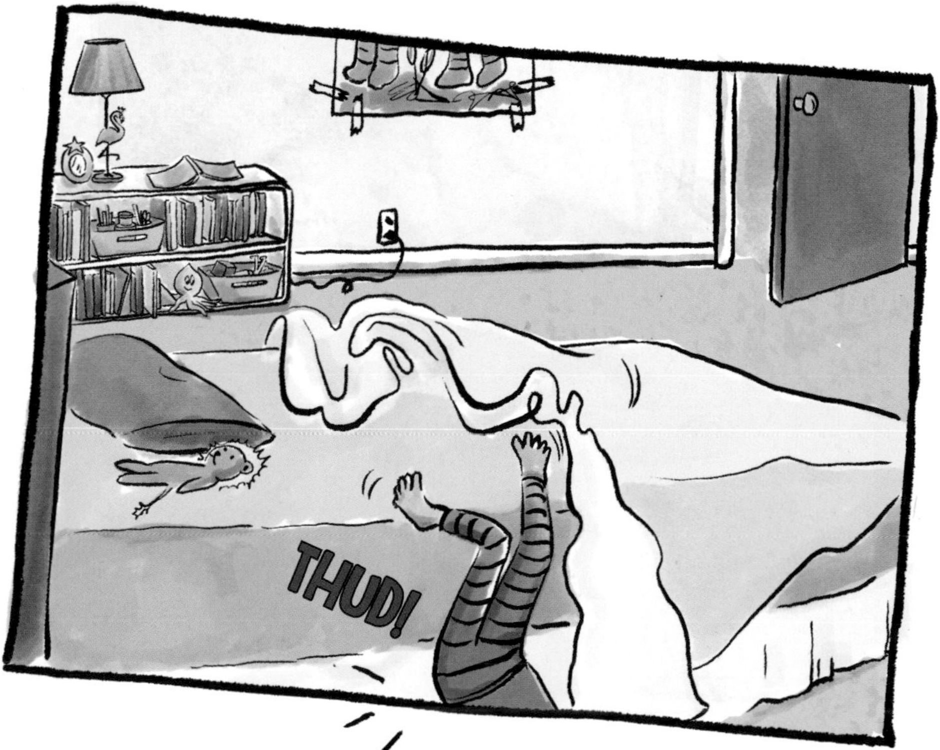
THUD!

Geraldine tries her best, but she's a bit tired.

At lunch Geraldine knows her stinky tofu will be stinky. So she sets Biandang down...

...far away from Nico.

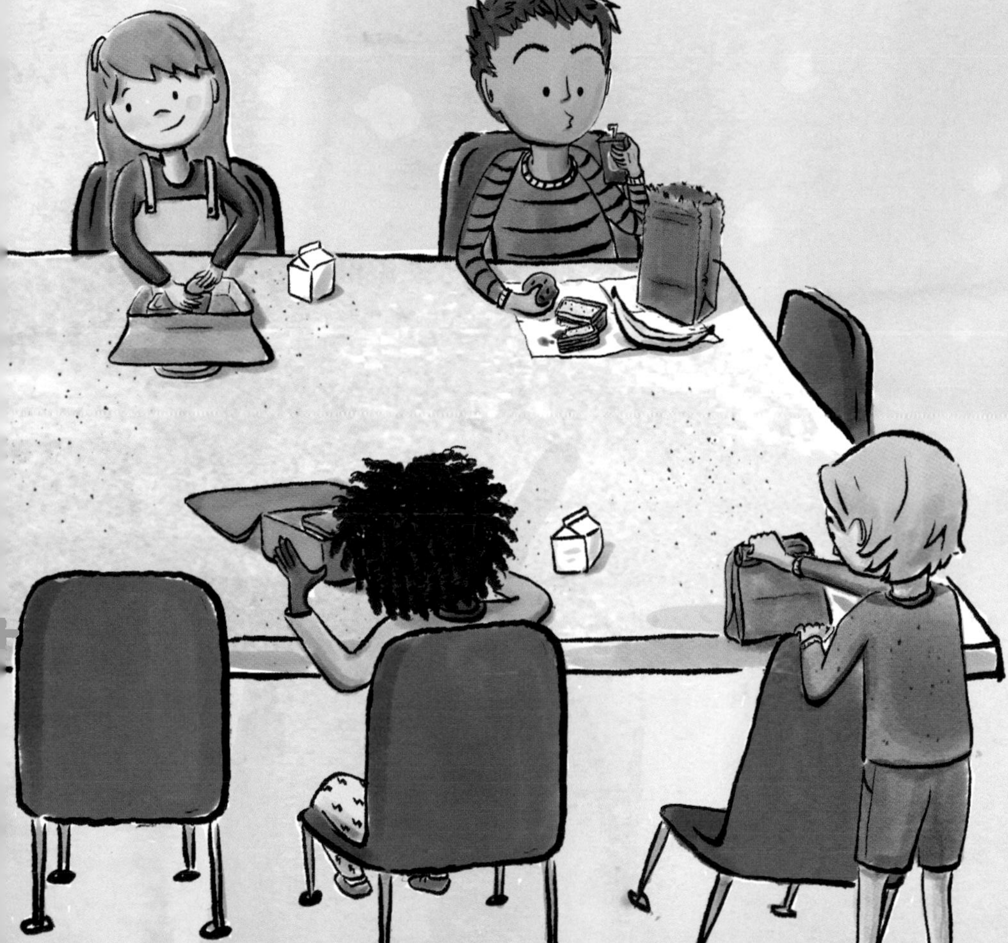

She takes a
deep breath...

...and unbuckles a buckle.

THWACK!

She goes to
unbuckle the
other side...

You got
this!

...when suddenly Nico exclaims,

Blech! That stinks!

Except he isn't talking to Geraldine!

He's talking to Deven—the boy from the bus!

Geraldine knows exactly how
Deven feels...

SCOOT

...and she knows
just what to do.

Chapter Four

Geraldine marches up to Deven and taps him on the shoulder.

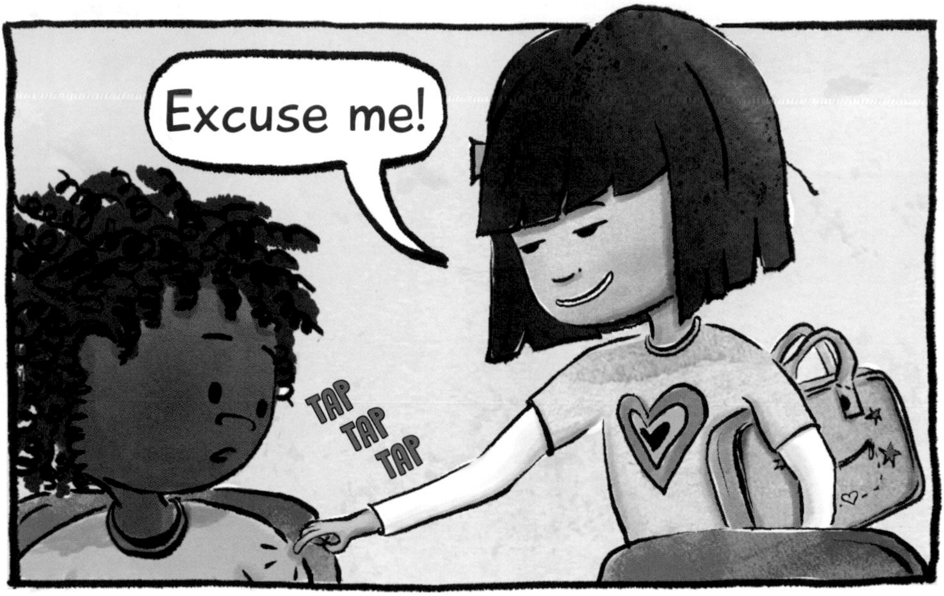
Excuse me!
TAP
TAP
TAP

She sits down with Biandang...

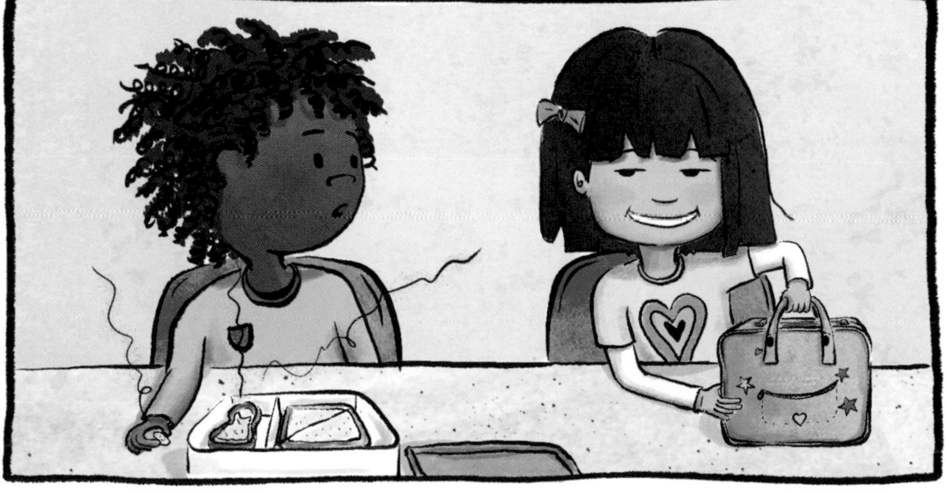

...clears her throat...

Everyone at the lunch table gasps.

Geraldine takes a bite and chews.

And chews.

And chews some more.

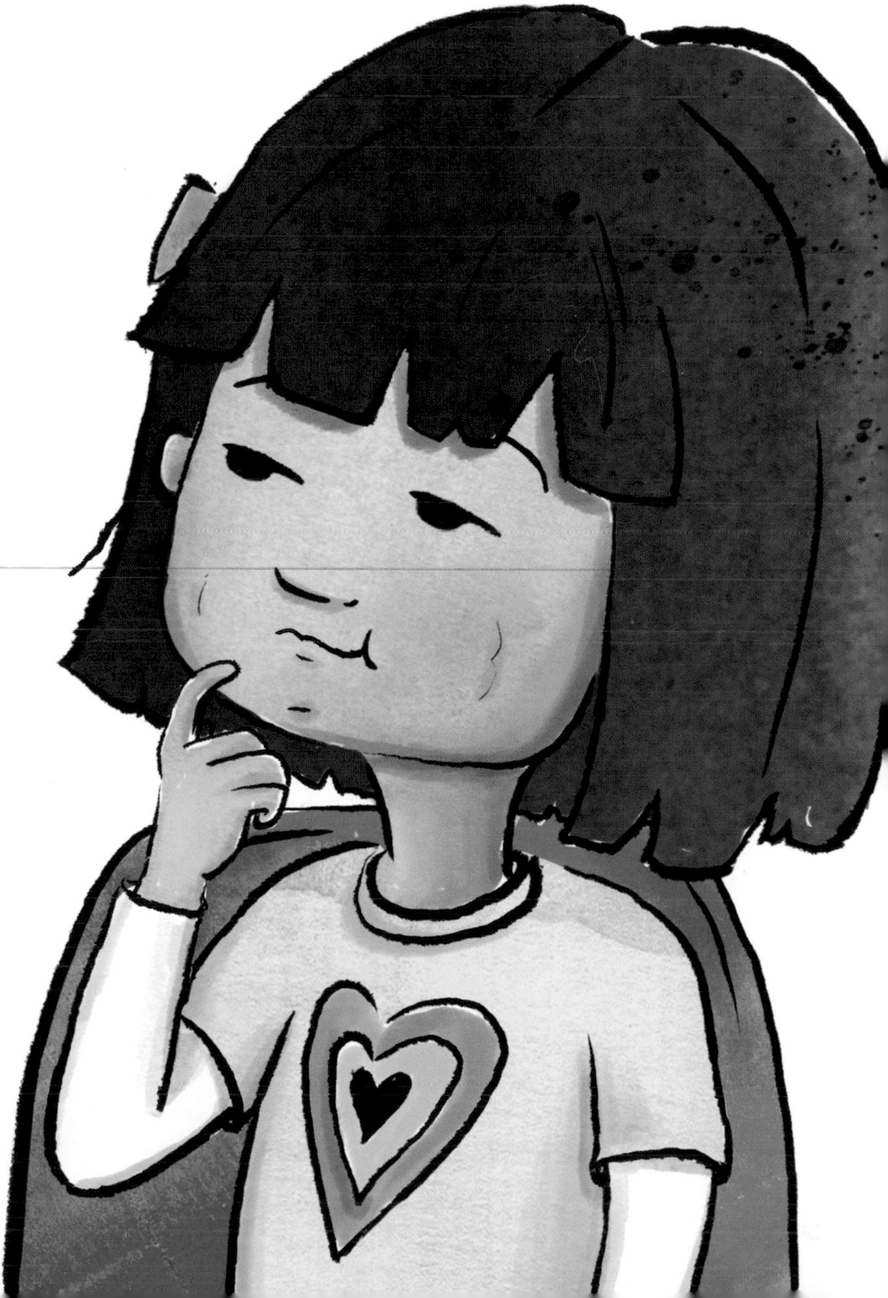

Then she gulps and says,

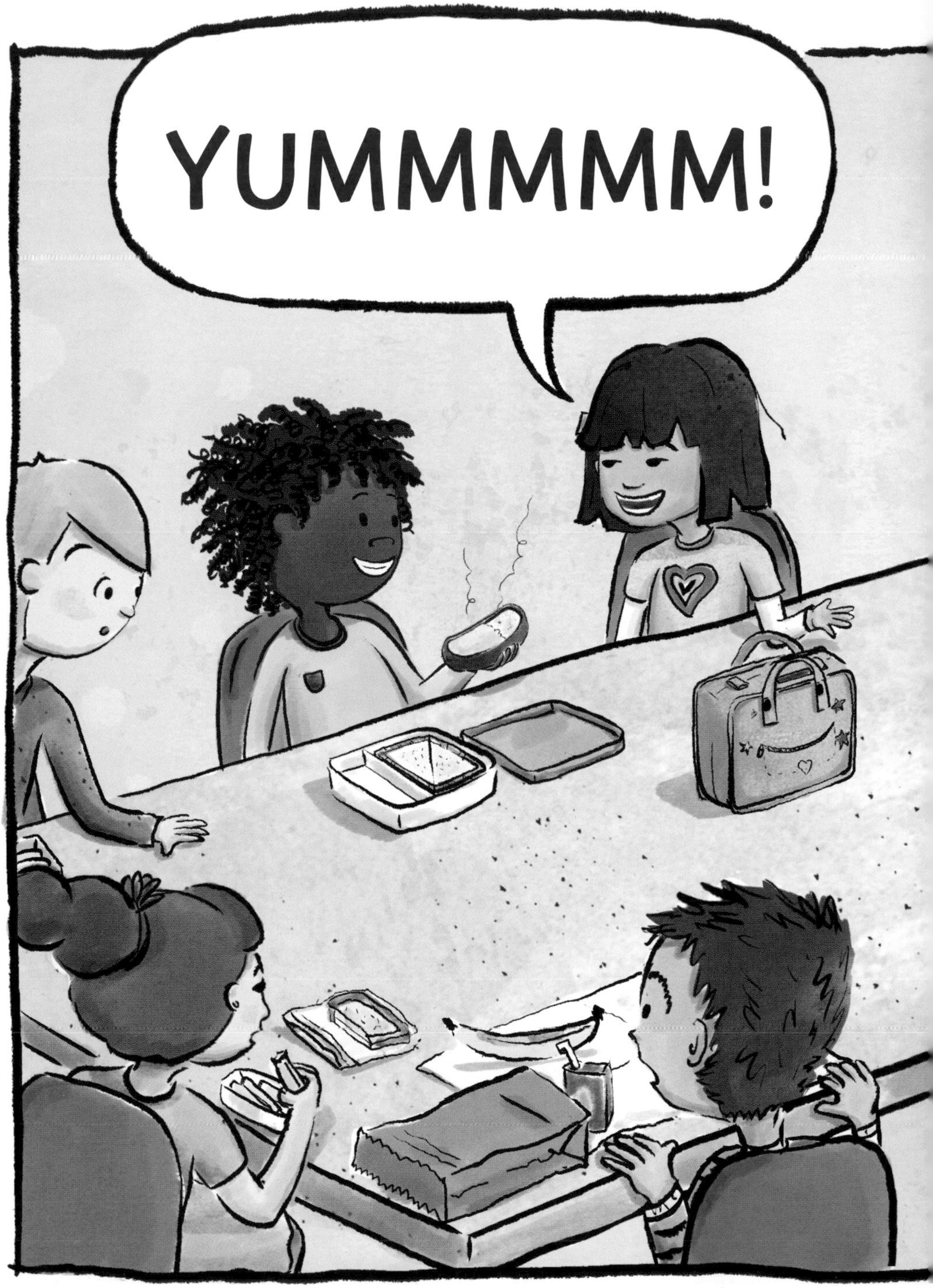
YUMMMMMM!

It's sweet, powdery, and REALLY tasty!

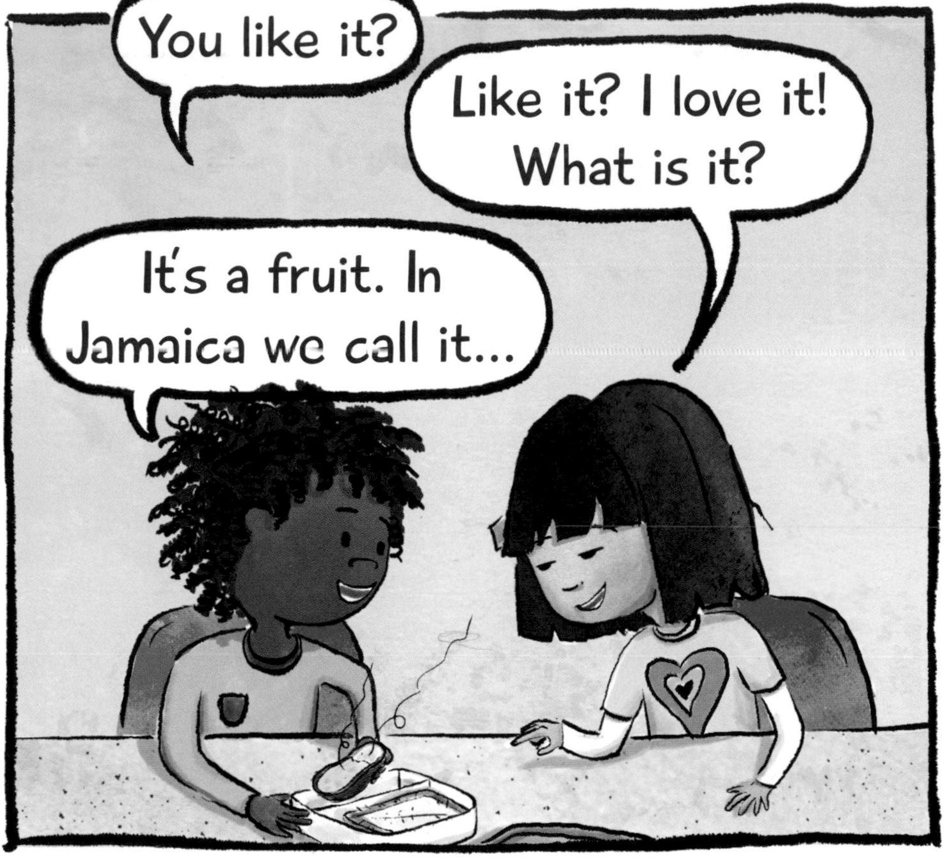
You like it?
Like it? I love it! What is it?
It's a fruit. In Jamaica we call it...

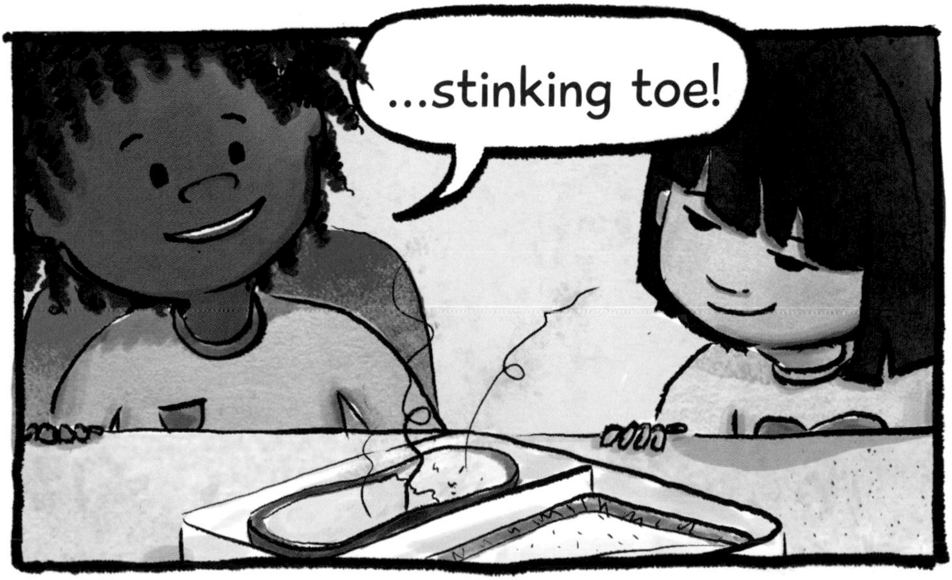
...stinking toe!

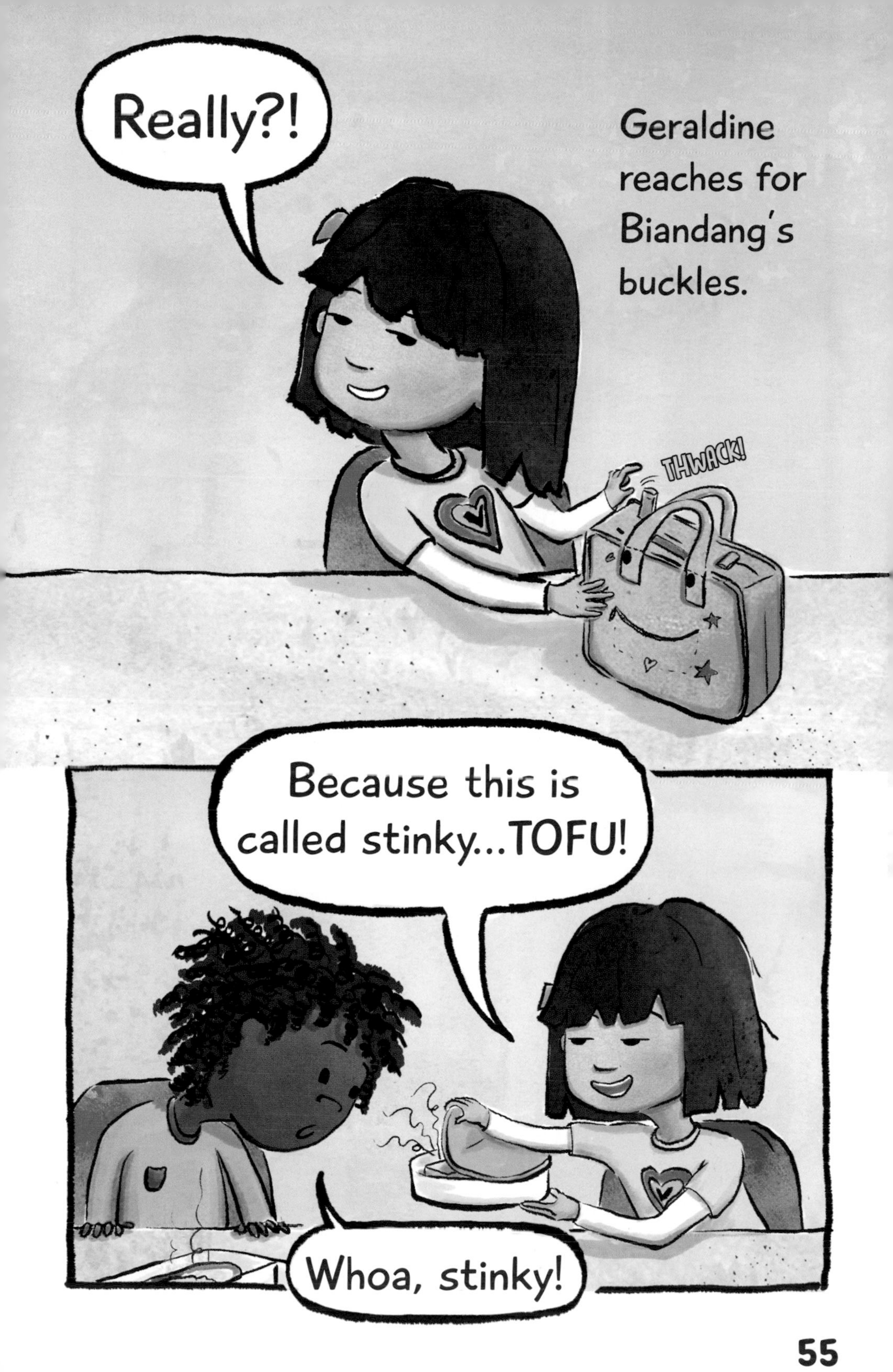
Really?!
Geraldine reaches for Biandang's buckles.
THWACK!
Because this is called stinky...TOFU!
Whoa, stinky!

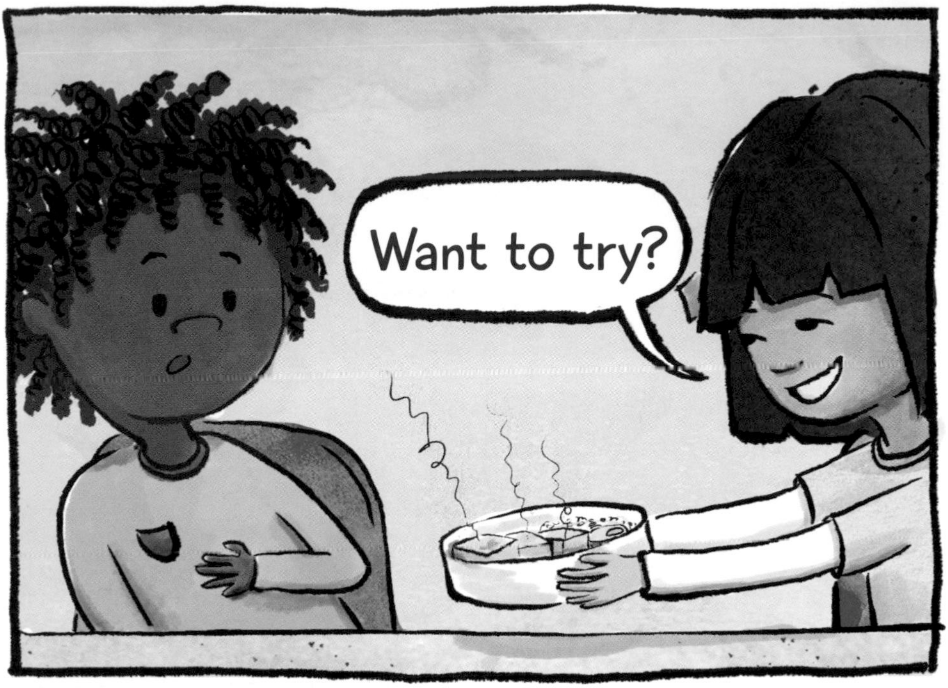
Want to try?

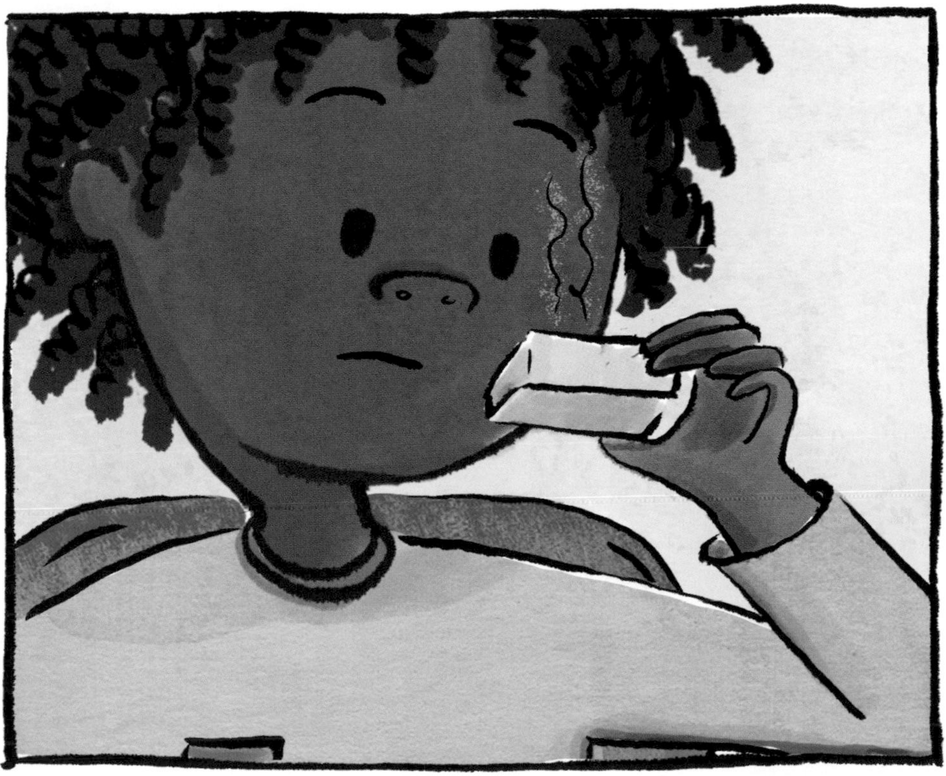

Deven takes a nibble and says,

Hey...pretty good!

And do you know how our girl Geraldine responds?

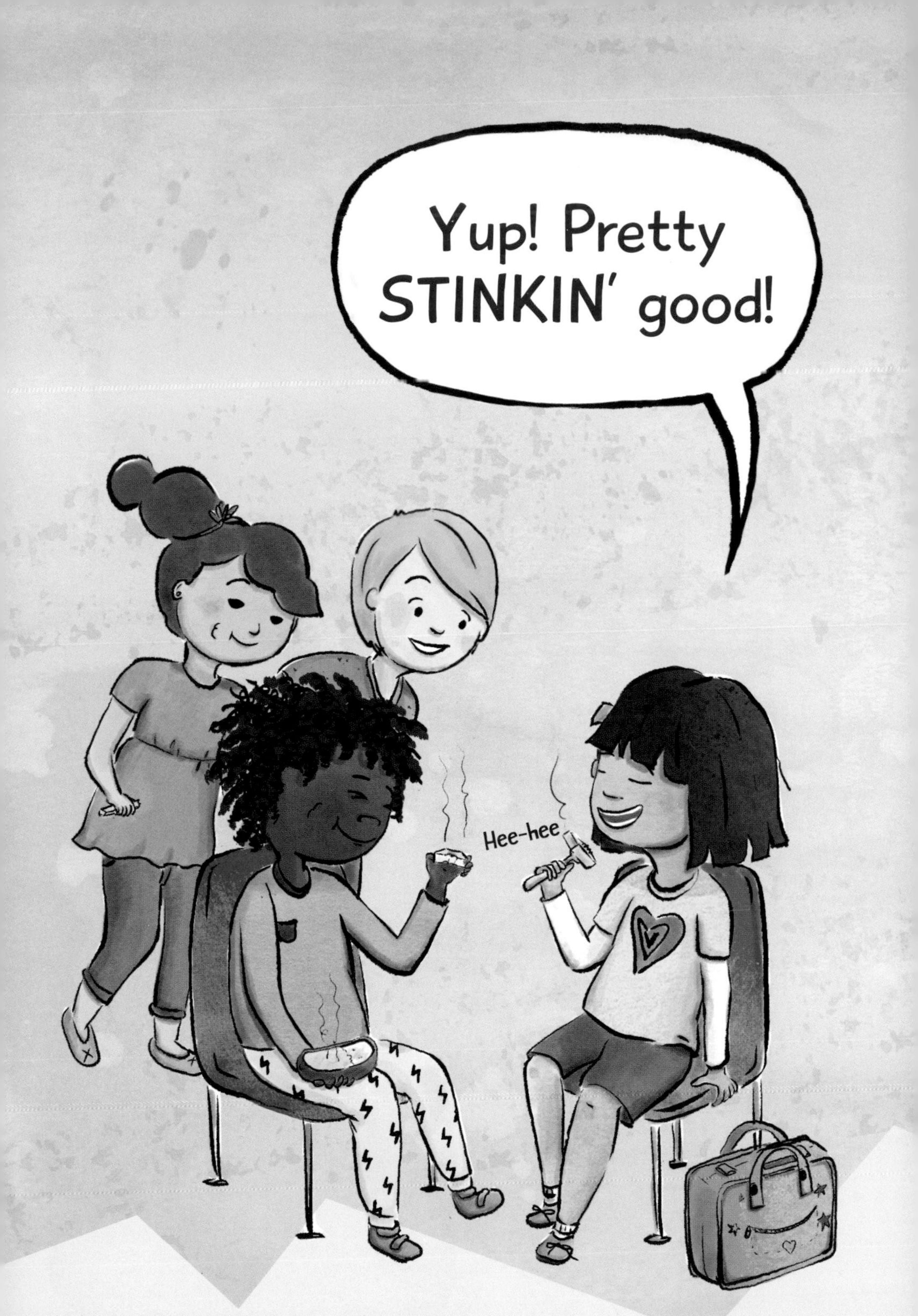
Yup! Pretty STINKIN' good!
Hee-hee

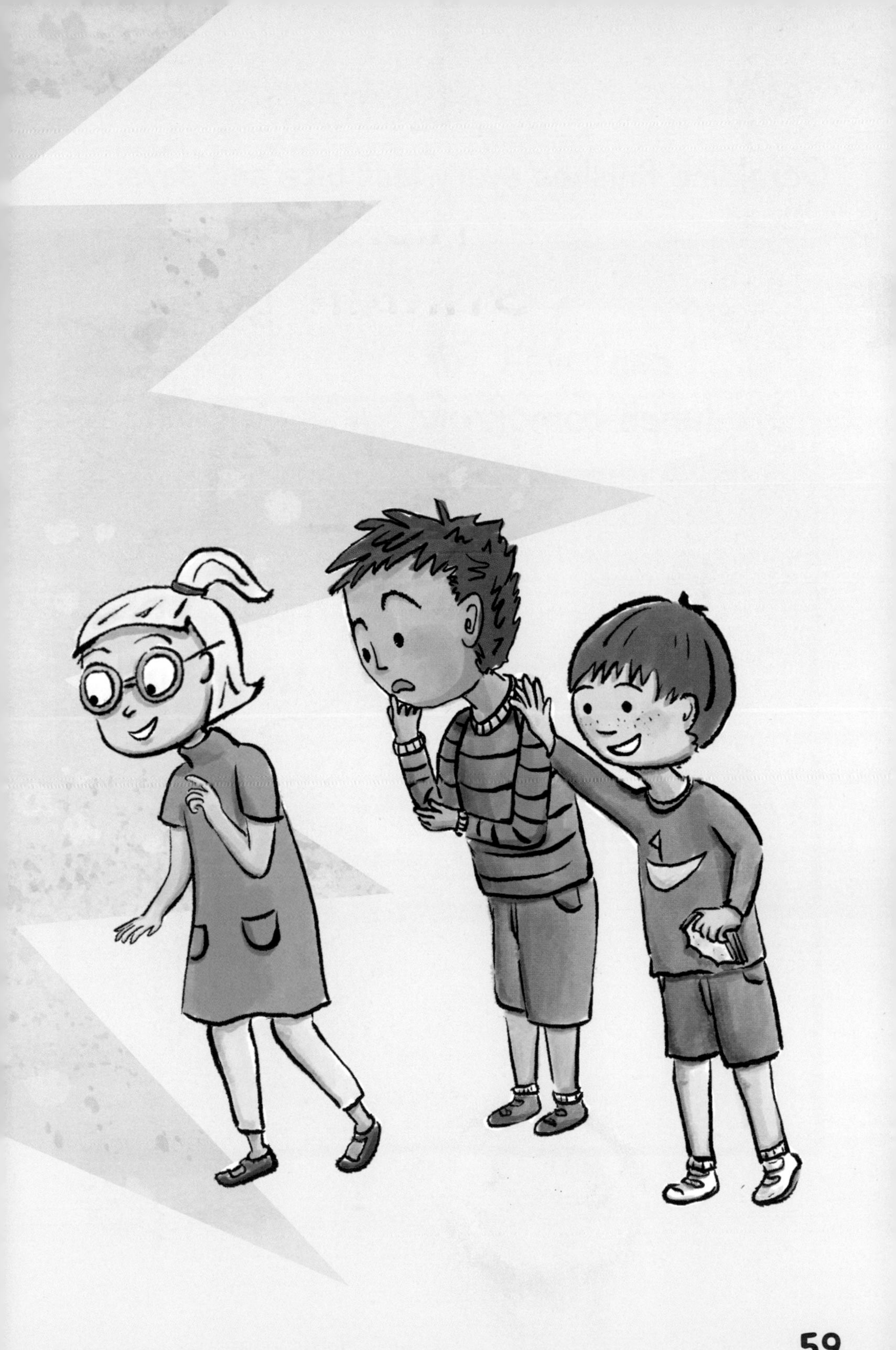

Geraldine finishes every last bite and says,

The End

A MESSAGE FROM BIANDANG

Pu is a real last name for people from Taiwan and China. Some names, or words, in one language can have a totally different meaning when spoken in another language. Like did you know that if you say "Ma" with just the right tone, you could be calling someone a horse in Mandarin Chinese?!

Also, stinky tofu is a real dish that is widely known in China and especially popular in Taiwan, where Geraldine and her family are from. While not everyone there is a fan of stinky tofu, many Taiwanese people do say, "The stinkier the tastier!" Stinking toe is also a real fruit. It is the chewy seedpod of one of the largest trees in the Caribbean. In fact, stinky foods are eaten all over the world! Like them or dislike them—either way is okay. Just be careful not to say "Yuck!" to someone else's "Yum!" and keep an open mind!

What new foods would you like to try?

AMAH'S STEAMED PORK BAO RECIPE

There are many ways to make a delicious bao. This is just one recipe you can try. It makes 12 baos and takes about 2 1/2 hours, but that includes waiting time!

Always prepare this recipe with a grown-up and use proper safety precautions.

INGREDIENTS

Dough
- 1 teaspoon active dry yeast
- 1 ½ teaspoons sugar
- 1 cup lukewarm water
- 3 cups all-purpose flour, divided, plus extra for dusting

Note: You'll also need parchment paper cut into 12 3-inch squares and a metal or bamboo steamer (but any steaming method will do).

Filling
- 1 pound ground pork
- 4 stalks of scallions (white and green parts), chopped
- ¼ teaspoon fresh ginger, finely minced
- 2 garlic cloves, minced
- ⅓ cup water
- 1 tablespoon oyster sauce
- 2 tablespoons soy sauce
- 2 tablespoons sesame oil
- ½ teaspoon salt
- ⅛ teaspoon white pepper
- 1 ½ teaspoons sugar

DIRECTIONS

1. In a large bowl combine yeast, sugar, and lukewarm water. Add just 2 cups of flour to start and mix with a fork. Then add about a 1/4 cup or less at a time of the remaining flour until the dough comes together, but is still a little sticky. (You might have flour left over after this.)

2. Dust a clean surface with flour. Knead dough by folding it in half and using only the palm of your hand to roll it away from you. Knead for about 7 to 9 minutes, lightly dusting with flour if dough sticks to your palm. The lumps will gradually smooth out as you knead, and you'll know you are done when the dough is completely smooth.

3. Tuck the edges of dough underneath itself to form a ball. Place into the bowl and cover with a damp kitchen towel. Set aside in the warmest part of your kitchen (about 75 to 85 degrees Fahrenheit) to rise for 1 to 2 hours or until doubled in size. Poke the dough and the dent should stay. If it springs back quickly, give it more time to rise. Make the filling while you wait.

4. In a bowl, combine all the filling ingredients. Use chopsticks (or fork) to stir until it has a paste-like consistency. Make sure to stir in only one direction or else you will have clumpy results.

5. Dust your surface with flour. Knead the dough for another few minutes to work out air pockets. Divide into about 12 even pieces and use your hands to roll each into a ball that's the size of an egg

6. Work with one dough ball at a time and keep the rest covered with a damp cloth towel. Dust a clean surface and a rolling pin or small cup with flour. Use the pin or cup to roll the ball into a circle where the edges are thinner than the middle. The circle should be about 4 1/2 inches in diameter with very thin edges.

7. Add 2 heaping tablespoons of filling to the center. Wrap the bao by pinching two opposite edges of the dough together. Then pinch the other opposite edges together. Tightly seal the "X" so you cannot see any filling. Pinch the four corners together to form a ball. Twist the tip to seal the bao.

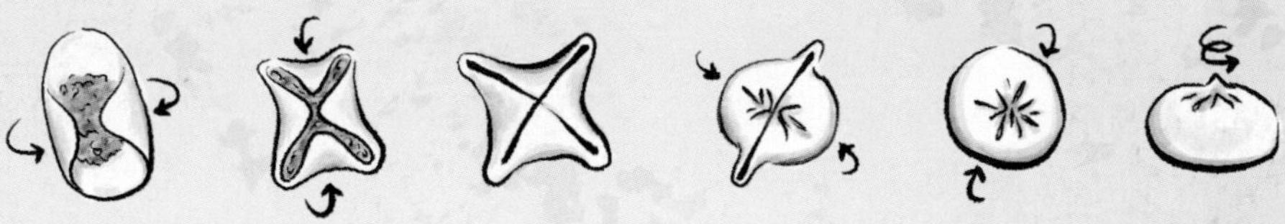

8. Lay the bao on a parchment paper square in the steamer, covered with a damp towel. Repeat Step 7, leaving 2 inches between the baos, until your steamer is full. (Try steaming a batch to test your results before wrapping the rest.)

9. Add 2 inches of water to a pan and bring to a boil over medium-high heat. Once the water boils, place the steamer on top of the pan, remove the damp towel, and cover with the lid. (If using a metal steamer, wrap the lid with the towel so no condensation drips onto the baos, and keep the towel away from the burner.) Steam for 15 minutes or longer, until fully cooked. The filling should be firm and no longer pink.

10. Serve warm and enjoy! Yummy!

STORING AND REHEATING TIPS

For best results freeze baos instead of refrigerating. Spread out cooked baos on a baking sheet and loosely cover them. Freeze for 1 hour, then transfer baos to a freezer bag. To reheat, cover the bao with a damp paper towel and microwave for 1 minute or until warmed throughout.